A new adventure from the duo that brought you
A Cat in a Kayak

A Seal in the Family

by Maria Coffey

illustrated by Eugenie Fernandes

Annick Press
Toronto • New York • Vancouver

For Dana, who grew up with Lucille.
M.C.

For the McKays, Bryna, Nathan, Jonas, John & Robyn.
E.F.

————————————

Readers are invited to visit Maria Coffey's Web site at: **www.island.net/~dagmaria/**

————————————

Annick Press Ltd.

We acknowledge the support of the Canada Council for the Arts for our
publishing program. We also thank the Ontario Arts Council.

We acknowledge the financial support of the Government of Canada through the Book
Publishing Industry Development Program for our publishing activities.

Cataloguing in Publication Data
Coffey, Maria, 1952-
A seal in the family

ISBN 1-55037-581-4 (bound)
ISBN 1-55037-580-6 (pbk.)

1. Harbor seal – Juvenile fiction. I. Fernandes, Eugenie, 1943- . II. Title.

PS8555.O2873S42 1999   jC813'.54   C99-930492-5
PZ7.C6585Se 1999

The art in this book was rendered in gouache.
The text was typeset in Seagull.

Distributed in Canada by:
Firefly Books Ltd.
3680 Victoria Park Avenue
Willowdale, ON
M2H 3K1

Published in the U.S.A. by:
Annick Press (U.S.) Ltd.
Distributed in the U.S.A. by:
Firefly Books (U.S.) Inc.
P.O. Box 1338, Ellicott Station
Buffalo, NY 14205

Printed and bound in Canada by
Friesens, Altona, Manitoba.

Teelo lived on Cloud Island, in a snug
little house filled with animals that Victor
the Vet had brought home in his kayak.

One summer afternoon, Teelo was on the beach waiting for Victor to paddle home from work, when he heard a strange sound. It didn't come from the seagulls flying by, or from the oyster catchers on the reef, or from the tug-boat motoring past Cloud Island. It was a sad, crying sound, and it came—Teelo stared in disbelief—it came from a rock!

Slowly, Teelo crept along the beach toward the rock that was crying so sadly. He stretched out a paw, but before he could touch it, the rock rolled over ...

... and he saw silvery whiskers, a gray speckled coat and soft brown eyes. This wasn't a rock at all, but a young seal pup. Teelo sat next to the pup, wondering where its mother was.

"Its mother has gone fishing," said Victor, when he paddled up. "Don't worry, she'll come back soon."

That night, as the moon rose over Cloud Island, things were peaceful inside the snug little house. Victor slouched on the sofa, reading a newspaper. Bonaparte the parrot perched beside him, preening his feathers. Terry the terrier lay in his basket, chewing a slipper. Sylvie the snake coiled on the windowseat, hissing happily. The hens nested in their box, cuddling up to Ruby the rooster.

Teelo couldn't settle in his usual place, under the wood stove. He sat outside in the moonlight, listening to the lonely cries of the seal pup as they drifted up on the breeze.

Next morning, the seal pup was still on the beach.

"Don't worry, its mother should come back soon," said Victor, as he paddled off to work.

All day, Teelo lay in a tree above the beach, looking out for the mother, who never came. When Victor paddled home that evening, he carefully examined the pup.

"She's very weak," he said. "Something must have happened to her mother, so she'd better come and live with us."

Inside the snug little house, Victor looked for a place to put the seal pup. He couldn't put her under the wood stove, because that was Teelo's spot. He couldn't put her in the dog basket, because Terry the terrier might chew on her flippers. He couldn't put her on the windowseat, because Sylvie the snake might squeeze her too tightly. He couldn't put her in the hen box, because Ruby the rooster might make a fuss. And he couldn't put her in the kitchen sink, because it was full of dirty dishes. So he put her in the bathtub.

"What shall we call this little seal?" he said. "How about Lucille?"

All the animals crowded around, admiring her silvery whiskers, her gray speckled coat and her soft brown eyes. And Teelo was pleased, because he was the one who'd found Lucille.

Suddenly, Lucille opened her mouth and gave an ear-splitting cry, for she was very, very hungry.

"Mah, mah, mah!" she cried, while Victor searched through his fridge and cupboards.

He found cheese and bread and peanut butter and ice cream and pickles, and dog food and cat food and chicken food and parrot food and snake food—but nothing that a baby seal could eat.

"Mah, mah, MAH!" she wailed, while Victor took his fishing rod off the wall, hurried down to his kayak and paddled out to sea.

"MAH MAH MAH!" she yelled, and she didn't stop until Victor rushed into the house with sculpins and shiners, which she gulped down in one big swallow.

At last, Lucille was quiet, and everyone fell asleep. As the moon rose over Cloud Island, all that could be heard inside the snug little house were gentle snores and the ticking of the clock. Until ...

"MAH! MAH! MAH! MAH!"

Lucille woke everyone with her cries that night, and the next night, and every night for weeks. She cried all day as well, and Victor had to dash home in his lunch hours to feed her, catching fish along the way. He was always tired and grumpy, he was too busy to shave or change his clothes, and he couldn't take a bath because Lucille was in the tub. He looked a mess! The house was messy too, with dustballs and fish bones all over the kitchen floor. Teelo was miserable, and wished he'd never found Lucille!

Lucille grew and grew, until Victor decided she was big enough to return to the ocean.

"It's where she belongs," he said, hoisting her out of the bathtub and carrying her down to the beach. "She'll be much happier there."

Lucille had forgotten about the ocean. When she saw the glittering water, she was terrified! As quick as her flippers would take her, she hauled up to the snug little house and flopped back into the bathtub.

"Don't be silly," said Victor. "Seals love to swim." He hoisted her out of the bathtub and carried her down the beach and right into the ocean.

Lucille had forgotten about swimming. When the waves lapped against her, she was terrified! As quick as her flippers would take her, she hauled up to the snug little house and flopped back into the bathtub.

"Seals are supposed to sleep outside," said Victor that
evening, hoisting Lucille out of the bathtub once more.
He carried her down to the beach and left her on a rock.

Lucille had forgotten about the moon. When it rose into
the sky above Cloud Island, she was terrified! As quick
as her flippers would take her, she hauled up to the snug
little house—but the door was shut and she couldn't get
to the bathtub. She lay on the step and cried all night,
keeping everyone awake.

"MAH MAH MAH!" wailed Lucille early next day, for she wanted her breakfast.

Victor hoisted her off the step and carried her down to the beach. Then he paddled away in his kayak, towing a fat fish on a long line.

"Here's your breakfast," he called to Lucille. "Come and get it!"

She saw the glittering water and felt the waves lap around her, but she was so hungry that she forgot to be afraid. She swam and swam after the fish, and gulped it down in one big swallow. Then she stopped swimming and looked about ...

She was far from shore, out in the glittering water, and big waves were lapping against her, but she wasn't terrified at all! She was so happy that she slapped her tail on the water. She dived under the kayak and came up the other side, twirling over to show Victor her belly. She snorted and splashed and cavorted—she was back where she belonged!

"Lucille lives in the ocean now," said Victor, when he paddled back to Cloud Island, "so things can get back to normal around here." He bathed and shaved and changed his clothes. He tidied up the kitchen and petted all the animals.

That night, as the moon rose over Cloud Island, things were subdued inside the snug little house. Victor slouched on the sofa, staring into space. Bonaparte the parrot perched beside him, sighing deeply. Terry the terrier lay in his basket, ignoring his slipper. Sylvie the snake coiled on the windowseat, hissing unhappily. The hens nested in their box, hunching up around Ruby the rooster.

Teelo couldn't settle in his usual place, under the wood stove. He sat outside in the moonlight, wondering where Lucille was, and if he'd ever see her again.

Several summers passed. One afternoon, when Teelo was on the beach of Cloud Island, he heard a familiar sound. It was a sad, crying sound, and it came from a rock. But as he crept toward the rock and reached out his paw, it turned over. This wasn't a rock at all, but a tiny seal pup.

Teelo sat by the pup, wondering where its mother was.

"Its mother has gone fishing," said Victor, when he paddled home from work. "Don't worry, she'll come back soon."

And very soon, a seal with silvery whiskers and a gray speckled coat and soft brown eyes hauled up the beach toward them as fast as her flippers would take her. It was Lucille! All the animals crowded around excitedly to greet her, and Teelo was pleased because he was the one who had found her pup.

Before too long, Lucille and her pup swam away. But the next summer, and each summer after that for years to come, Teelo found a new seal pup on the beach of Cloud Island. He never wondered where its mother was, because he knew Lucille had gone fishing, and that she'd come back very soon.

photo: Eugenie Fernandes

The Real Lucille

This story is based on a real-life harbor seal, who lives off the coast of British Columbia, Canada. A man found her on the beach and presumed she was abandoned, when in fact her mother had probably just left her for a while to go fishing. The man brought her to some marine biologists who knew how to look after a seal pup, and she survived.

If you find a seal pup all alone on the beach, please don't disturb it, as it is probably waiting for its mother to return. If it is still there after forty-eight hours, call your local veterinarian, who will know the right thing to do.

Things to Know about Harbor Seals

Harbor seals, like Lucille, are found in the oceans of the Northern Hemisphere. Their life span is twenty-five to thirty-five years, and they grow to be about 100 kilograms (220 lbs.) in weight.

Female harbor seals begin breeding when they are four years old, and they have one pup a year. They feed their pups with special seal milk, which is very rich and fatty. To produce enough of this milk, the mothers must eat lots of fish. When they go fishing, they usually leave their pups alone for a while.

The pups stay with their mothers for about a month. Once they are weaned off milk, they begin eating fish and they leave their mothers to live independently.